WEEKLY WR READER
EARLY LEARNING LIBRARY

Nature's Food Chains

What River Animals Eat

by Joanne Mattern

Reading consultant: Susan Nations, M.Ed.,
author/literacy coach/consultant

Science and curriculum consultant: Debra Voege, M.A.,
science and math curriculum resource teacher

Please visit our web site at: www.garethstevens.com
For a free color catalog describing Weekly Reader® Early Learning Library's list
of high-quality books, call 1-877-445-5824 (USA) or 1-800-387-3178 (Canada).
Weekly Reader® Early Learning Library's fax: (414) 336-0164.

Library of Congress Cataloging-in-Publication Data

Mattern, Joanne, 1963-
　　What river animals eat / by Joanne Mattern.
　　　　p. cm. — (Nature's food chains)
　　Includes bibliographical references and index.
　　ISBN-10: 0-8368-6874-9 — ISBN-13: 978-0-8368-6874-6 (lib. bdg.)
　　ISBN-10: 0-8368-6881-1 — ISBN-13: 978-0-8368-6881-4 (softcover)
　　1. Stream animals—Food—Juvenile literature.   2. Food chains (Ecology)—
Juvenile literature.   I. Title.   II. Series: Mattern, Joanne, 1963- Nature's food chains.
　　QL145.M38　　2007
　　591.764—dc22　　　　　　　　　　　　　　　　　　2006009183

This edition first published in 2007 by
Weekly Reader® Early Learning Library
A Member of the WRC Media Family of Companies
330 West Olive Street, Suite 100
Milwaukee, WI 53212 USA

Editor: Barbara Kiely Miller
Art direction: Tammy West
Cover design, page layout, and illustrations: Dave Kowalski
Picture research: Diane Laska-Swanke

Picture credits: Cover, title, p. 15 © Tom and Pat Leeson; p. 5 © David Kjaer/naturepl.com;
p. 7 © Duncan McEwan/naturepl.com; p. 9 © Bill Beatty/Visuals Unlimited; p. 11 © Gary Meszaros/
Visuals Unlimited; p. 13 © Jorma Luhta/naturepl.com; p. 17 © Joe McDonald/Visuals Unlimited;
p. 19 © Kenneth Lucas/Visuals Unlimited

Printed in the United States of America

1 2 3 4 5 6 7 8 9 10 09 08 07 06

Note to Educators and Parents

Reading is such an exciting adventure for young children! They are beginning to integrate their oral language skills with written language. To encourage children along the path to early literacy, books must be colorful, engaging, and interesting; they should invite the young reader to explore both the print and the pictures.

The *Nature's Food Chains* series is designed to help children learn about the interrelationships between animals in a food chain. In each book, young readers will learn interesting facts about what animals eat in different habitats and how food chains are connected into food webs.

Each book is specially designed to support the young reader in the reading process. The familiar topics are appealing to young children and invite them to read — and reread — again and again. The full-color photographs and enhanced text further support the student during the reading process.

In addition to serving as wonderful picture books in schools, libraries, homes, and other places where children learn to love reading, these books are specifically intended to be read within an instructional guided reading group. This small group setting allows beginning readers to work with a fluent adult model as they make meaning from the text. After children develop fluency with the text and content, the book can be read independently. Children and adults alike will find these books supportive, engaging, and fun!

— Susan Nations, M.Ed., author, literacy coach,
and consultant in literacy development

All living things need food to live and grow. Some animals eat plants. Some eat smaller animals. These ducks belong to a river food chain. A **food chain** shows the order of who eats what.

Plants are at the bottom of food chains. They make their own food using sunshine, water, and air. Many animals that live in or near rivers eat plants. This small insect eats water plants.

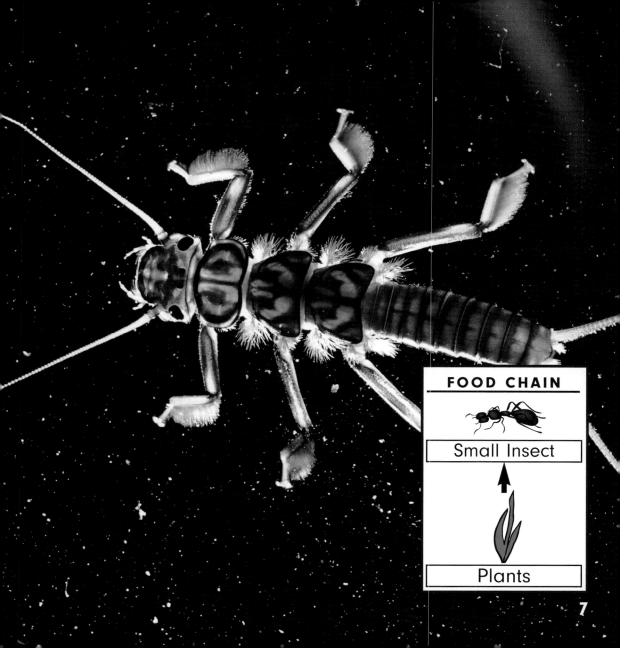

FOOD CHAIN

Small Insect

Plants

Small insects are eaten by bigger insects. A **dragonfly** eats this small insect.

FOOD CHAIN

Dragonfly

↑

Small Insect

↑

Plants

Then the dragonfly is eaten by a frog.
Frogs eat many kinds of insects.

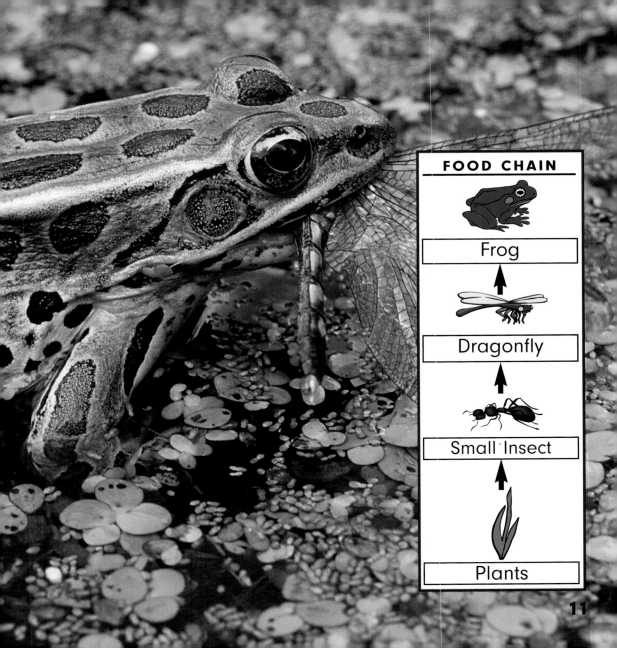

FOOD CHAIN

Frog

↑

Dragonfly

↑

Small Insect

↑

Plants

Bigger animals eat frogs. Snakes eat frogs. This **river otter** is eating a frog. An adult river otter is at the top of its food chain. No other animal eats it.

FOOD CHAIN

Snake

River Otter

Frog

Dragonfly

Small Insect

Plants

13

A river has many food chains. The plants at the bottom of river food chains are eaten by many animals. This duck eats plants.

FOOD CHAIN

Duck

↑

Plants

Larger animals eat ducks. An alligator eats this duck. Alligators are at the top of their food chains.

FOOD CHAIN

Alligator

Duck

Plants

An animal or a plant can be part of more than one food chain. This alligator eats ducks. But it eats frogs, insects, and snakes, too! Eating many kinds of foods helps animals stay alive.

A **food web** is formed when two or more food chains are connected. Animals that are part of more than one food chain connect the chains. Food webs show that animals have many things to eat!

A River Food Web

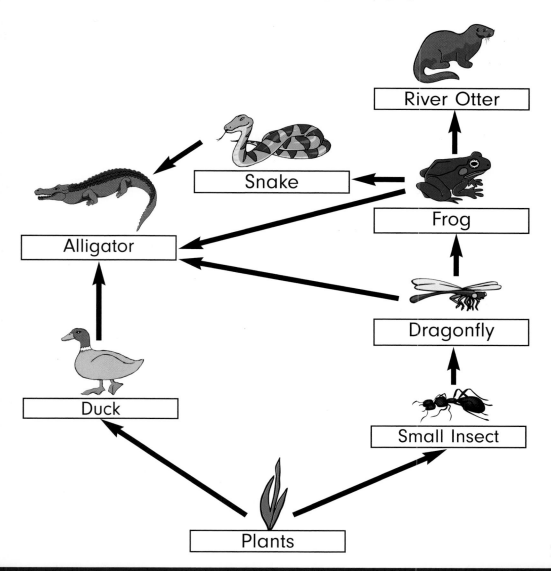

Glossary

dragonfly — a large insect with a long body and four narrow, clear wings

food chain — a list of living things, in which each plant or animal is eaten by the next animal on the list

food web — food chains that are connected by a plant or animal that is common to both chains

river otter — an animal with thick fur and webbed feet that lives in or near water.

For More Information

Books

The Life Cycle of a Dragonfly. Things with Wings (series). JoAnn Early Macken (Gareth Stevens)

River Otter at Autumn Lane. Smithsonian's Backyard (series). Laura Gates Galvin (Soundprints)

Rivers. Water Habitats (series). JoAnn Early Macken (Gareth Stevens)

Who Eats Who in Rivers and Lakes. Food Chains in Action (series). Andrew Campbell (Franklin Watts)

Web Site

Chain Reaction
ecokids.earthday.ca/pub/eco_info/topics/frogs/chain_reaction
Play a game to put a food chain together. Find out what happens when one part of the chain is gone.

Publisher's note to educators and parents: Our editors have carefully reviewed this Web site to ensure that it is suitable for children. Many Web sites change frequently, however, and we cannot guarantee that a site's future contents will continue to meet our high standards of quality and educational value. Be advised that children should be closely supervised whenever they access the Internet.

Index

About the Author

Joanne Mattern has written more than one hundred and fifty books for children. Joanne also works in her local library. She lives in New York State with her husband, three daughters, and assorted pets. She enjoys animals, music, going to baseball games, reading, and visiting schools to talk about her books.